There are more books
about Pokémon.

Collect them all!

#1 I Choose You!

#2 Island of the Giant Pokémon

#3 Attack of the Prehistoric Pokémon

#4 Night in the Haunted Tower

coming soon

#5 Team Rocket Blasts Off!

movie novelizations

Mewtwo Strikes Back

Pikachu's Vacation

Movie Adaptation by
Tracey West

SCHOLASTIC INC.
New York   Toronto   London   Auckland   Sydney
Mexico City   New Delhi   Hong Kong

ISBN 0-439-13741-1

12 11 10 9 8 7 6 5 4 3 2   9/9 0 1 2 3 4/0

Printed in the U.S.A.
First Scholastic printing, November 1999

Welcome to the world of Pokémon! To help you enjoy the movie *Pokémon: Mewtwo Strikes Back* (and this book based on the movie), here's a little Poké "cheat sheet." It's all you need to know in a nutshell — or a Poké Ball!

CHARACTERS

Ash Ketchum. On his tenth birthday, Ash became a Pokémon trainer — someone who captures and takes care of Pokémon. Ash's team of Pokémon includes Pidgeot, Muk, Tauros, Lapras, Bulbasaur, Charizard, Squirtle, and of course, Pikachu.

Brock. An experienced trainer, Brock used to be a Gym Leader, but when he met Ash, he decided to join him on his journey to capture more Pokémon. Brock wants to learn as much as he can about raising strong, healthy Pokémon. He likes to travel with his Pokémon, Geodude, Onix, Zubat, and Vulpix.

Giovanni. The sinister leader of the Team Rocket empire, Giovanni's goal is to one day rule all the world's rare and powerful Pokémon.

Mew. This legendary Pokémon has never been seen alive — until some scientists discovered Mew's fossilized eyebrow and used it to create Mewtwo.

Mewtwo. Cloned from the fossilized eyebrow of Mew, Mewtwo is angry with the scientists who created it.

Misty. Born in beautiful Cerulean City, Misty specializes in training Water Pokémon. She travels around with Ash and Brock. Misty takes along Starmie, Staryu, Goldeen, Seadra, and Psyduck.

Pikachu. Ash was shocked when he got this Electric Pokémon the day he became a Pokémon trainer. Now Pikachu is more than just Ash's Pokémon — it's a good friend.

Pokémon. "Pocket Monsters," as they are called, are creatures that come in all shapes, sizes, and personalities. Pokémon trainers capture Pokémon and train them to face other Pokémon in battle. Most Pokémon can evolve into more advanced forms of Pokémon by gaining battle experience or by being exposed to special stones. There are at least 151 Pokémon in the world — and trainers are finding new types of Pokémon all the time!

Team Rocket. A trio of Pokémon thieves made

up of a teenage girl named Jessie, a teenage boy named James, and their talking Pokémon, Meowth. They're under orders from Giovanni to steal rare Pokémon — including Pikachu. So far, they haven't had much luck!

TYPES OF POKÉMON

While all Pokémon are different, they can be grouped according to several basic types. A Pokémon's type determines what special powers it will have in battle. Some Pokémon are a combination of more than one type.

    1. **Bug.** These creepy crawly creatures look like insects — but they're much bigger than the ones you're used to!

    2. **Dragon.** They may look like the dragons in fairy tales, but these Pokémon have abilities you've never read about.

    3. **Electric.** With thunderbolts and other electric attacks, these Pokémon are shockingly good in battle!

    4. **Fighting.** These pumped-up Pokémon pack a powerful punch!

    5. **Fire.** These flame-shooting Pokémon are too hot to handle!

6. **Flying.** These Pokémon often have the advantage, because they can attack in midair.

7. **Ghost.** Besides being spooky, these Pokémon are notoriously hard to catch.

8. **Grass.** These Pokémon usually look like animals, but they have vines, leaves, and other plant parts that they use in battle.

9. **Ground.** These sturdy Pokémon like to live close to, even under, the ground.

10. **Ice.** The freezing powers of these Pokémon have a chilling effect on their opponents.

11. **Normal.** They're called Normal because they don't have any powers associated with elements like fire or water. These Pokémon are often the most unusual of all!

12. **Poison.** It's not easy to recover when one of these Pokémon poisons you during an attack.

13. **Psychic.** These Pokémon use special mind powers, such as telekinesis, to control the movements and actions of their opponents.

14. **Rock.** They're made of stone, tough as nails, and hard to beat!

15. **Water.** These Pokémon usually live in water, and use water attacks when they battle other Pokémon.

POKÉ STUFF

Poké Ball. A red-and-white ball that trainers use to capture and hold Pokémon. The Pokémon are released when the trainer throws the ball or pushes a button on the ball.

Pokédex. A handheld computer that trainers carry. It holds information about all of the world's Pokémon.

Our Story Begins . . .

Many know of the ancient legend. Millions of years ago, a deadly storm wiped out all but a few Pokémon. The magical tears of those Pokémon rained down on the planet. All life on Earth was restored by those Pokémon tears.

Now it is millions of years later, and a new, very different life is about to be created. A new legend is about to be born. . . .

Prologue

COMPUTER DIARY OF PROFESSOR JOHN SMITH

POKÉMON CLONING LABORATORY

NEW ISLAND

January 1
Our colleagues made an exciting discovery deep in the Amazon jungle today! They found a fossilized eyebrow in a cave. Near the fossil was an ancient cave drawing of the legendary Pokémon, Mew. No one has ever seen a Mew alive. Mew is reputed to have amazing powers, even for a Pokémon. If this fossil does prove to belong to Mew, we may have a chance to make scientific history.

March 14

We spend hours in the lab each day, barely eating or sleeping. We have isolated Mew's DNA. As soon as we perfect the cloning machine, we can begin to attempt a clone of Mew. Won't it be wonderful to create new life from something that has been extinct for so long? It will be like giving a gift to the world.

June 4

Arguments among the scientists. Some members of the team want to alter Mew's DNA to make the cloned Pokémon even more powerful. Others say we should leave the DNA just as it is. But how can we pass up the chance to improve on what nature has created? If we don't try to make the Mew clone more powerful, we won't be living up to our potential as scientists.

July 15

All agree to alter Mew's DNA. This clone could be the most powerful creature in the world. We are about to undertake the greatest experiment ever.

August 31

The DNA has been altered. The cloning machine is ready. We will attempt the cloning process tonight.

September 3

The cloning process was successful! The Mew clone is asleep in a tank of fluid in the laboratory. We will call it Mewtwo. There is nothing to do now but watch and wait for it to wake up. Watch and wait . . .

Chapter One

Mewtwo Awakes

Strange images floated through the Pokémon's mind. Bubbles dancing in crystal blue water. An island somewhere in the middle of the ocean. A small creature without wings flying through the air.

And humans. Many humans.

The Pokémon stirred slowly. It opened its eyes. It was floating in a glass tank filled with red fluid. A group of humans surrounded the tank. Humans in long white coats. Scientists. They were staring at it and whispering.

"It's awake!" one of the scientists cried.

Awake . . . I'm awake. The Pokémon looked down at its body. Strong muscles tensed beneath its white fur.

It did feel awake. It felt more than awake. It felt powerful.

The Pokémon closed its eyes and imagined the tank breaking into a million pieces. Almost instantly, the tank around it shattered. Red fluid spilled onto the floor.

The Pokémon crouched on the floor. "Where am I?" the Pokémon asked. Its deep, rich voice filled the room. "*Who* am I?"

One of the scientists stepped forward.

"Mewtwo is complete!" the man said.

"Mewtwo?" the Pokémon asked.

"That's your name," said the scientist. "We used the rarest Pokémon in the world to create you. It is called Mew."

The man pointed to an image on a computer screen. It was an ancient drawing. It looked like it might have been scratched on a cave wall. The drawing showed a catlike Pokémon. The creature looked like Mewtwo, but smaller. It had big eyes and a long, thin tail.

Mewtwo's eyes narrowed. This was the creature from its dreams.

"You said you used Mew to create me. What did you mean?" Mewtwo asked.

The man beamed. "It's a scientific miracle! We used a sample of Mew's DNA to make a copy of Mew — a clone. You are the result of our experiment."

"Why?" Mewtwo asked. "Why did you do it?"

"We wanted to see if it was possible to make a clone of the legendary Mew," the scienist said. "We proved it could be done."

Confusion clouded Mewtwo's brain. The humans seemed so pleased with their work. But Mewtwo didn't feel like a scientific experiment. It felt alive.

"And now what will you do with me?" Mewtwo asked.

"We will study you," the scientist replied. "We believe you are stronger than Mew. We would like to find out exactly what you are capable of."

Anger filled Mewtwo. *These scientists only created me to run tests on me,* Mewtwo thought. *They treat me like an object. But I am not an object. I am alive.*

"I will show you what I am capable of!" Mewtwo said angrily.

Mewtwo's eyes narrowed. The room was filled with more large tanks of red fluid. Mewtwo concentrated on those first.

Crash! Mewtwo caused the tanks to shatter — just by *thinking* about it. The humans screamed in terror. Some began to flee the room.

Their screams delighted Mewtwo. Next it concentrated on the computer screen. Instantly, electric sparks shot from the machine. Soon the room was in flames.

"Mewtwo, no!" a scientist cried. He frantically reached for a button on the wall.

Mechanical arms shot out from the walls and surrounded Mewtwo. Mewtwo countered by shooting blue light from its eyes. The light formed a giant blue bubble around Mewtwo.

The bubble carried the Pokémon clone safely out of the burning room and out of the building. Mewtwo noticed that the building was a laboratory of some kind.

Once outside, Mewtwo saw that the lab was on a small island.

Below, angry red flames shot up from the lab. A feeling of power surged through Mewtwo like a jolt of electricity. It felt good.

Mewtwo floated in the bubble and landed on the island's rocky shore. Mewtwo dissolved the bubble. Someone was coming.

A deafening noise filled the air. Looking up, Mewtwo saw a helicopter flying overhead. The helicopter landed on the shore.

A large man in a dark suit emerged from the helicopter. He carried a tan Pokémon that looked like an exotic cat. *A Persian,* Mewtwo thought, without knowing exactly how it knew.

"You're as powerful as I thought," the man said. "If you come with me, I'll show you how to use that power. Together, we can control the world."

Why should I trust a human? Mewtwo thought. But this man was different from the scientist. *He said we could control the world. He knows I am more than an experiment. He knows how powerful I am. Perhaps he can help me.*

"Who are you?" Mewtwo asked.

"My name is Giovanni. I lead Team Rocket," the man said.

A leader. A powerful man like this would have much to offer.

Mewtwo nodded. "I will come with you."

Mewtwo climbed into the helicopter. As they flew away, the Pokémon watched the lab explode in an orange ball of fire.

Chapter Two

Mewtwo Is Tested

Metal clamps tightened around Mewtwo's wrists and ankles.

The Pokémon was in Giovanni's lab, in a remote mountain region. The human had promised Mewtwo more power than it had ever dreamed of.

But the human had a strange plan.

"We must control your power or you will destroy the world and everything in it," Giovanni had explained. "This armor will protect your body and focus your power. If we control your power, we can use it to take over the world."

Mewtwo was reluctant at first. But Giovanni had to be smart to get where he was. This human must know what he was doing. *I will go along with him for now,* Mewtwo thought. *I will see what he does.*

So Mewtwo had agreed to sit in this large metal chair. Mewtwo sat calmly as the clamps tightened. Now plates of shiny silver armor emerged from the chair. They tightened around Mewtwo's arms. Its legs. Its chest. Even its head.

"You can still use your power," Giovanni said.

"What will I do with it?" Mewtwo asked.

Giovanni's eyes gleamed. "You will fight!"

The Team Rocket leader pressed a silver button. A door opened. A giant Pokémon waited behind the door. It looked like a huge snake made of stone. Mewtwo's psychic powers told him that this Rock Pokémon was called Onix.

Before Onix could attack, Mewtwo concentrated on sending a Psychic Blast in its direction.

Slam! The Rock Pokémon tumbled to the ground. Mewtwo had defeated it in an instant.

"Excellent," Giovanni said, stroking the Persian cat in his lap. "But we need more tests. More battles."

Each day Mewtwo faced off against different Pokémon, each more powerful than the last.

Each time, the Pokémon clone was victorious.

Nothing could stop it.

Mewtwo faced a herd of Tauros on an open field. The bull-like Pokémon charged at Mewtwo with their sharp horns. Mewtwo focused, causing a whirlwind to spin below their feet. The wind sent the helpless Tauros flying into the air.

Mewtwo faced Alakazam, the foxlike Pokémon that some said had the strongest abilities of all Psychic Pokémon. It held two spoons, symbols of its amazing psychic power. Alakazam didn't even have a chance to strike. Mewtwo aimed Psychic Waves of blue light at Alakazam. The psychic force bent the two spoons. Alakazam was defeated.

Mewtwo faced Magneton, an Electric Pokémon made up of three joined silver balls and powerful electric magnets. Magneton threw a blast of magnetic energy at Mewtwo. Mewtwo reversed the blast. The energy surrounded Magneton, sending it crashing to the floor.

Not even Nidoking and Arcanine could defeat Mewtwo. Nidoking, a Poison Pokémon covered with sharp spikes, and Arcanine, an agile Fire Pokémon, charged Mewtwo at full force. A single blast of light sent the two flying into the air, defeated.

One by one, Giovanni sent Pokémon to battle Mewtwo. And one by one, Mewtwo defeated them.

At first, Mewtwo didn't mind the tests — it almost enjoyed them. But as the days went by, it began to wonder what Giovanni had in mind.

"Tell me, human," Mewtwo said. "What am I fighting for?"

Mewtwo and Giovanni were in the lab. Giovanni sat on a balcony high above the lab floor.

Giovanni looked down on Mewtwo and smiled.

"You are fighting for me, of course," Giovanni said. "Every Pokémon needs a human master."

"A human master?" Mewtwo asked. "But I thought we were going to rule the world as equals."

Giovanni laughed. "Equals? That's impossible," he said. "Humans created you. You can never be equal to us."

Mewtwo stared at Giovanni. *This human wants to control me,* Mewtwo thought. *But look how far away from me he sits. He is afraid of me.*

"You're right. I'm not a human," Mewtwo said. "And I was not born a Pokémon. I was created. And my creators have used and betrayed me."

The thought upset Mewtwo. But instantly, his sadness turned to anger.

Sparks flew from Mewtwo's armor.

"I don't need a human to help me control the world," Mewtwo declared. "I can do it on my own!"

Giovanni watched in horror as Mewtwo's eyes glowed with eerie blue light. The armor flew off Mewtwo's body.

That's when Giovanni realized what had just happened.

The Pokémon's full power was unleashed!

"Humans may have created me," Mewtwo cried, "but they will never enslave me!"

A blue bubble surrounded Mewtwo's body. Mewtwo floated high into the air. The Pokémon focused its psychic energy, sending an explosive charge speeding through the lab.

The explosion rocked the ground below it. The bubble burst, and Mewtwo flew away like a speeding comet.

It was time to start again.

Mewtwo flew over the ocean. It landed on the island where it was created. The laboratory lay around him in ruins. No matter. It would rebuild it.

Mewtwo looked out over the sea.

"Soon I will have my revenge," it said. "My revenge on all humans!"

Chapter Three

Ash Ketchum, Pokémon Trainer

Ash Ketchum sat down on a patch of green grass. He lifted his cap and ran his fingers through his brown hair.

"I'm tired," Ash said, "and hungry. Let's stop here. I can't take another step."

Ash's friend Misty shook her head. "Some Pokémon trainer you are, Ash. You haven't caught any new Pokémon in weeks."

Ash grimaced. Ever since his tenth birthday, Ash had been on a journey as a Pokémon trainer. One day he hoped to become the best Pokémon master in the world.

But to do that, he'd have to catch and train lots of Pokémon.

"Every Pokémon trainer needs to rest once in a while," said Brock, an experienced Pokémon Gym Leader who was traveling with Ash and Misty. "I think we should stop, too. It's a nice spot."

Relieved, Ash leaned back and put his arms behind his head. It *was* a nice spot, Ash thought. They were on a high cliff that overlooked the ocean. The air smelled clean and salty.

"Pika! Pika!" Ash's Pokémon, Pikachu, hopped up on Ash's knees and smiled. An Electric Pokémon, Pikachu was bright yellow with pointy ears and a tail shaped like a lightning bolt.

"I guess you like it here, too, huh, Pikachu?" Ash asked.

"Pika pi!"

A tiny Pokémon hopped up next to Pikachu. It was Togepi, a rare Pokémon that had hatched from an egg that Ash found. Togepi still carried the bottom half of the eggshell around its little round body. Its tiny head popped out from the top of the shell. Tiny arms and legs stuck out from the sides and bottom.

"*Togi, togi!*" chirped Togepi in a high voice.

Pikachu jumped off Ash and ran to play with Togepi. Misty had opened up her backpack and was setting up a picnic lunch. Her red hair gleamed in the afternoon sunlight. Brock had started a small fire and was busy cooking Pokémon food in a small pot.

I'll just take a little nap, Ash thought. He pulled his cap over his eyes.

Ash's eyes were barely closed when a loud voice boomed through the clearing.

"Ash Ketchum!"

Ash sat up. An older teenage boy walked up to their campsite. Ash thought he looked kind of like a pirate. A scarf covered his black hair. He wore a vest with no shirt underneath. Attached to the vest were red-and-white Poké Balls.

"Are you Ash Ketchum, the Pokémon trainer from Pallet Town?" the boy asked.

Ash jumped to his feet. "That's me!"

"How about a battle?" the trainer challenged.

Ash grabbed a Poké Ball from his belt. "If you're looking for a battle, you've found one!"

Misty shook her head. "I thought you couldn't take another step," she said.

"A Pokémon battle is a piece of cake," Ash said confidently.

"Be careful," Brock warned. "This guy looks tough."

Ash and the trainer faced each other on the open grass. The trainer grabbed a Poké Ball from his vest. He threw the ball.

"Poké Ball, go!" the trainer cried.

There was a burst of white light, and a Pokémon appeared. It was a Donphan, one of the newly discovered Pokémon. It stood on four sturdy legs. Two curved horns extended from its head. Silver armor covered its body.

"Go, Poké Ball!" Ash cried, and threw his ball. "Bulbasaur, I choose you!"

Bulbasaur appeared in another burst of light. It looked like a small dinosaur with a plant bulb growing out of its back.

Donphan started the attack. It begin to spin furiously in the air, forming a wheel with its body. It sped at Bulbasaur. With a crash, it knocked into Bulbasaur and sent it flying into the air.

Bulbasaur was shaken but landed on its feet.

"Bulbasaur, Solarbeam!" Ash commanded.

The plant bulb on Bulbasaur's back opened slightly. Tiny, shimmering plant spores floated out. Then a bright beam of light shot up from the bulb. Bulbasaur aimed the beam at Donphan.

The Solarbeam slammed into Donphan. The Pokémon fainted and collapsed in a heap on the ground.

"You won the first round, Ash!" Brock called out.

Ash smiled and hugged Bulbasaur.

Angrily the trainer recalled Donphan and took another Poké Ball from his vest. He threw the ball, and a Machamp appeared.

Ash knew the trainer wasn't playing around. Machamp was a tough Fighting Pokémon with a muscular gray body and four powerful arms.

"Bulbasaur, take a rest," Ash said. He threw another Poké Ball.

"Squirtle, I choose you!" Ash cried.

A Water Pokémon that looked like a turtle appeared. Squirtle almost looked too cute to defeat Machamp, but Ash knew Squirtle could do it.

Machamp flew at Squirtle, aiming punches with all of its arms. Squirtle used its agility to dodge the punches.

"Squirtle, Bubblebeam!" Ash called out.

Squirtle opened its mouth. Powerful water bubbles shot out and slammed into Machamp.

The bubbles were too much for Machamp. It fainted.

"Way to go, Squirtle!" Ash said. He happily lifted Squirtle into the air.

Brock and Misty cheered. "That's two for you, Ash," Brock called out.

The trainer's face was beet-red.

"I'm not finished with you yet!" he cried.

The trainer threw three Poké Balls into the air.

A Pinsir appeared. A large Bug Pokémon, Pinsir had two curved claws on top of its head that could inflict a lot of damage.

A Venomoth appeared. This flying Bug

Pokémon had a poisonous sting. Not many challengers could recover from its poison attacks.

A Golem appeared. This Ground Pokémon looked like a turtle made of rocks. It was almost impossible to damage it in a battle.

"These guys are hard to beat," Brock said. "Ash, what are you going to do?"

The trainer glared at Ash.

"Pinsir! Venomoth! Golem!" he called out. "Attack!"

A Mysterious
Invitation

"Pikachu, I choose you!" Ash yelled.

"Pikachuuuuuuu!" Pikachu jumped high in the air.

Jagged bolts of lightning exploded from Pikachu's body. Pikachu hurled the lightning at the attacking Pokémon.

Zap! Pinsir collapsed in a heap.

Zap! Venomoth plummeted to the ground.

Zap! Golem crashed into Pinsir and Venomoth.

The battle was over.

"I did it!" Ash cried. Pikachu jumped into Ash's arms.

The trainer recalled his Pokémon and stomped away.

Misty shrugged. "He was a weak opponent."

Ash frowned. "Can't you just admit that I'm getting good?"

Brock stepped between them. "That opponent did need a little more training," Brock said, "but Ash, you *are* getting to be a good trainer. Now let's eat!"

The friends sat down and began to eat a feast of sandwiches and Pokémon food. No one noticed the Flying Pokémon that soared above them.

It was a Fearow. The large, birdlike Pokémon had a video camera strapped around its neck. It was sending images of Ash's Pokémon battle to a video screen on an island in the middle of the ocean.

Mewtwo's island.

Mewtwo watched the images of the battle on the screen. *This one is strong,* Mewtwo thought. *A worthy opponent.*

Mewtwo gestured with its pawlike hand.

A large Pokémon appeared — a Dragonite. It looked like a dragon with a round snout and small wings on its back.

Mewtwo slipped a small, flat box into a pouch on the Dragonite's back. The Dragonite flew out of the window and across the ocean.

Mewtwo wasn't the only one watching Ash's Pokémon battle. A teenage girl with long red hair and a teenage boy with short dark hair spied on Ash from high on a nearby ledge. A small, catlike Pokémon stood next to them.

It was Jessie, James, and their Pokémon, Meowth. A trio of Pokémon thieves known as Team Rocket, they were intent on stealing Pikachu. So far, they'd had no luck.

James watched Pikachu through a pair of binoculars. "That was a great battle," James said. "Pikachu keeps getting better and better."

"We'll get that Pikachu someday," Jessie said.

"That's right!" Meowth said. "We don't know the meaning of the words 'give up.'"

"What are they doing now?" Jessie asked James.

James's stomach rumbled. "They're eating. It looks delicious," he said. His stomach rumbled again. "I'm so hungry."

"We can't catch Pikachu on empty stomachs," Jessie said. She handed Meowth a frying pan. "Meowth, make us some lunch!"

"But we have no food," Meowth said. "I can't make lunch out of thin air."

"Speaking of thin air," James said, "watch out!"

The large Dragonite came speeding down from the sky.

Whoosh! Dragonite knocked over Team Rocket.

Next, Dragonite swooped down and flew into Ash's picnic area. Dust clouded the air as Dragonite skidded to a stop.

Ash gazed in wonder at the large orange Pokémon. Dragonite reached into the pouch on its back and pulled out the small, flat box. It handed the box to Ash.

The lid of the box flipped open automatically. A round laser disk began to whir.

Suddenly, a three-dimensional image of a woman appeared.

"Whoa, she's beautiful," Brock said.

"She's a hologram," Ash said.

The hologram began to speak. "This message is for highly promising Pokémon trainers. I invite you to a party hosted by my master, the world's greatest Pokémon trainer. It will be held at the Pokémon Palace on New Island."

The image of the woman disappeared. In its place was a map. The map showed a small island surrounded by ocean.

A white envelope fluttered out of Dragonite's pouch.

The woman appeared again.

"There is a ferry waiting at the wharf to take all trainers to New Island," she said. "Use the postcard to reply." Then she disappeared for the last time.

Pikachu picked up the invitation and handed it to Ash. It had two boxes printed on it — one for Yes and one for No.

"I don't get it," Misty said. "Who sent this?"

"The world's greatest Pokémon trainer," Ash said. "I wonder who he is?"

"Or *she*," Misty pointed out.

"I don't care who sent it," Ash said. "It feels good to be called a highly promising Pokémon trainer."

"And that woman in the hologram was *so* beautiful," Brock said. He had a dreamy look in his eyes. "We have to go."

Misty took the postcard from Ash. "Okay, then. I'll check off Yes."

Misty put the postcard back in Dragonite's pouch.

They watched the large Pokémon fly away.

"This is going to be great," Ash exclaimed. "Let's go to the wharf!"

Dragonite flew back up into the sky, past the ledge overlooking Ash and his friends — and right into Team Rocket.

Jessie and James pushed on Dragonite's nose.

"Hold it right there," James commanded.

Jessie took the invitation from Dragonite's pouch.

"A gathering of 'highly promising Pokémon trainers,'" Jessie read. "Think of all the Pokémon that will be there!"

James's eyes gleamed. "So many Pokémon for us to steal!"

"*Meowth!* I think we've got a party to crash," Meowth said.

From its island tower, Mewtwo looked out at the calm ocean. It slowly raised its paw and made circles in the air.

Any human to oppose me must be worthy, Mewtwo thought. *I must make it so that only the strongest humans will reach New Island.*

At Mewtwo's command, the ocean waves began to rise and fall. Dark storm clouds gathered in the sky. Freezing rain poured from the clouds.

Come to me, Mewtwo thought, pleased at the growing storm he was creating. *Come to me — if you can.*

Far away, something was brewing in different waters.

A Pokémon lay sleeping in a pink bubble at the bottom of a bright blue pool.

The Pokémon stirred.

It opened one eye.

"Mew," said the Pokémon.

The pink bubble began to gently float up through the water. The bubble reached the surface and burst, sending Mew flying gracefully into the sky.

Mew knew where it had to go. There was a rocky island in the middle of the ocean. Something there needed it.

Mew had a job to do.

Braving the Storm

Freezing rain pelted Ash as he ran down the wharf with Pikachu in his arms. Misty ran next to him carrying Togepi, and Brock was right behind them.

Crack! A bolt of thunder shook the sky.

"We're not going to make it!" Ash shouted.

A building stood at the end of the wharf.

"That must be the wharf house," Brock said. "We're almost there."

Ash struggled against the rain and wind

to reach the safety of the shelter. With an exhausted grunt he pulled open the door.

The door opened into a large room with many windows that overlooked the wharf. Ash couldn't believe his eyes. The room was crammed with Pokémon trainers and their Pokémon.

"Look, there's a Kingler!" Ash said, pointing to a large, crablike Pokémon with sharp claws. A yellow Pokémon with black lightning bolts on its body sped by. "Cool! An Electabuzz."

A loud voice carried over the clatter in the room.

"What do you mean, the ferry's not going out?"

Ash spun around. A young female police officer named Jenny was blocking the entrance to the ferry dock. Next to her was an older woman in an official-looking blue suit.

The voice belonged to a tall, stocky Pokémon trainer with short black hair. He wore a red tank top and yellow shorts. Ash thought he looked like a surfer.

"I am Fergus, one of the greatest Pokémon trainers in the world," he said. "I have to get to that island. I have an invitation!"

A pretty teenage girl with shoulder-length brown hair stepped up next to Fergus. "He's not the only one. I'm going to that island, too."

"You're not keeping me away, either," said another trainer. This one was a skinny older boy with messy dark hair.

Me too, Ash said silently to himself.

Officer Jenny held up her hands. "Settle down, everyone. This woman is in charge of the wharf."

The woman in the blue suit stepped forward. "My name is Miranda. I know these waters better than anyone. And I can tell you right now that no one is going anywhere. I've never seen a hurricane as bad as this. It's as bad as the legendary storm."

Ash turned to Brock and Misty. "Legendary? What legend?"

"Ash, don't you know anything?" Misty asked. "She's talking about the legend of the storm at the beginning of time."

Brock nodded. "It's an old story. A storm wiped out all life on Earth, except for a few

Pokémon. In their sorrow, the remaining Pokémon wept. Their tears rained down on the world and restored the lives lost in that storm."

"Pokémon tears? That's the craziest story I've ever heard," Ash said.

Fergus folded his arms defiantly. "A storm doesn't scare me. I can handle it."

Miranda shook her head. "As the guardian of this port, I can't send you off into such danger."

"I'm sorry, but the ferry will *not* be crossing," Officer Jenny said firmly.

Ash's heart sank. Going to this island seemed like it could be his most exciting adventure ever. And now it was over even before it began.

Ash scanned the faces of the other trainers. Most of them looked disappointed — but some just seemed more determined than ever.

Fergus took a Poké Ball from his pocket.

"No problem for my Pokémon. They're all strong in water," Fergus bragged. "Just watch me cross this ocean!"

Fergus hurled the Poké Ball past Miranda's head, over the dock, and into the water.

A Gyarados appeared in a blaze of light. This Water Pokémon resembled a giant sea serpent.

The appearance of the Gyarados startled Miranda and Jenny. Fergus saw his chance. He sped past them and jumped onto Gyarados's back.

"So long!" he yelled as he rode off into the storm.

"Wait!" Miranda called after him. "If your Pokémon get injured, there's no way to help them. The Pokémon Center is closed."

"What do you mean?" Ash asked.

Officer Jenny pointed to a poster on the wall. It was Nurse Joy. She and her cousins took care of injured Pokémon at Pokémon Centers all over the world.

"Nurse Joy disappeared one week ago," Officer Jenny explained. "No one knows where she is."

Brock gazed at the poster. "She's so beautiful," he said dreamily. "You know, she looks familiar. Like I've seen her somewhere before."

Misty sighed. "Brock, of course you've seen her before. There's a Nurse Joy in every city. They all look the same."

Brock didn't seem to hear her. "She's so beautiful," he repeated.

Suddenly, the sound of flapping wings filled the air.

Ash looked up. The skinny trainer was flying out into the storm on a Flying Pokémon — a Pidgeotto. The brown-haired girl was also making a break for it. She ran out onto the dock and jumped on the back of a Dewgong, a white Water Pokémon.

Officer Jenny ran after them. "Stop! Or you're under arrest!" she called out.

Miranda put an arm on Officer Jenny's shoulder. "There's no way to stop them. They're Pokémon trainers — adventurers. If they were quitters, they wouldn't be here in the first place."

Determined, Ash turned to Brock and Misty. "I'm no quitter, either!"

Ash ran out onto the dock. The rain lashed at his face. The stormy waves rose and fell against the black sky.

"We've got to get to the island," Ash said.

"There's no way," Brock said. "It isn't safe to make our Pokémon carry us there. You heard what Officer Jenny said. If they're injured, there's no Pokémon Center. It's not right."

Ash stared down at his sneakers. "You're right, Brock. I guess there's nothing we can do."

"Excuse me, sir, but are you looking to cross these waters?"

Ash snapped to attention. A large wooden boat had pulled up to the dock. Two people were rowing the boat. They were dressed like Vikings in furs and hats with horns on them. On the front of the boat was a figurehead of a Viking maiden with braids and a long gown.

Ash blinked. The figurehead looked strangely like a cat. A catlike Pokémon.

"So would you like a ride or not?" one of the Vikings asked.

Ash eyed the boat suspiciously. "Can this thing really make it?"

"I have trained in the waters of the Amazon," the Viking said. "Rough waters are my specialty."

Ash turned to his friends. "Let's do it! It's our only way!"

"*Pika?*" Pikachu looked nervous.

"It looks dangerous," Misty said. She held Togepi tightly. "But I really want to go to the island, too."

"All right, then," Brock said. "All aboard!"

Ash and his team climbed into the boat and sat on wooden benches.

The Vikings used long oars to row the boat. The waves were rough. The boat bounced up and down, up and down on the rocking waves.

"These are the roughest waves I've ever seen," Misty remarked.

Suddenly, the ship's figurehead spoke. "They're about to get rougher! Look!"

A giant wave towered high above them. There was no escaping it. The wave crashed down on the boat.

Salt water stung Ash's eyes. When he opened them, he saw that the water had washed away the Vikings' hats and furs.

Surprise! They weren't Vikings at all!

"Team Rocket!" Ash cried. He looked at the figurehead. "And Meowth!"

Jessie grinned an evil grin. "That's right," she said. "Prepare for trouble. . . ."

". . . and make it —" James began.

"There's no time for that!" Meowth cried. "Another tidal wave is coming!"

Ash braced himself as a second wave, larger than the first, crashed on the boat. This wave was just too powerful.

Ash struggled to hold on. It was no use.

The wave turned the boat upside down, plunging them all into the stormy ocean.

Chapter Six

New Island

Ash grabbed Pikachu as the force of the wave sent them deep into the ocean.

Ash knew they couldn't survive the rough waters on their own. Reaching for his belt, Ash pulled off a Poké Ball and pushed a button. Squirtle, his Water Pokémon, appeared.

Ash and Pikachu held onto Squirtle's back. There wasn't much time. His lungs felt like they would burst.

Squirtle swam up to the surface. Ash and Pikachu gasped for air. Rain lashed at their faces. Ash struggled to keep his head above water.

Misty and Brock's heads were above the water, too. They were hanging onto Misty's Starmie, a Water Pokémon that looked like a large starfish.

"These waves are too rough!" Ash called out over the roar of the ocean.

"We'll have to go underwater!" Misty called back.

Ash knew she was right. If they stayed on the rough surface, the waves would keep pounding them. They'd never get anywhere.

Ash took a deep breath of air, then dived with Squirtle and Pikachu under the waves. Misty and Brock swam ahead of them.

The black waters churned and heaved around them. Squirtle fought against the strong current to swim forward.

Ash held on as long as he could. But he needed air.

He tapped Squirtle's back. Squirtle nodded and swam back to the surface. Misty's Starmie did the same.

Cold air filled Ash's lungs. He opened his eyes.

All at once *calm* water surrounded them. No waves crashed against them. No rain fell from the sky.

Ash looked up. He and his friends were inside a wide circle of whirling winds. But the sky above them was clear and calm. A full moon shone brightly overhead.

"We're in the eye of the storm," Misty said.

"We're safe for now," Ash said, "but what's next?"

Pikachu pointed ahead. *"Pika pi."*

A dim yellow light burned through the foggy darkness. It wasn't far away.

"That could be coming from New Island!" Ash said excitedly.

"There's only one way to find out," Brock said. He began to swim in the direction of the light.

Swimming in the calm water was much easier than swimming in the storm. The light grew brighter and brighter.

Soon Ash could make out a long

wooden dock jutting out into the water. The light was coming from a lantern.

Ash and the others swam closer. Now Ash could see a figure holding the lantern. It was a woman.

The woman from the hologram!

Ash climbed up onto the dock and pulled Pikachu and Squirtle up with him. Misty called to Starmie and stood on the dock, cradling a frightened Togepi. Brock stared at the woman holding the lantern.

She wore a white box-shaped hat and a long, old-fashioned red dress with puffy sleeves. Red hair hung in long braids down her back.

"So you have arrived," the woman said in a soft, dreamy voice. "Please show me your invitation."

Ash took the flat box out of his dripping wet knapsack. "You mean this?"

The box opened, and the hologram appeared.

"These trainers have come here by invitation," the hologram said. "You may let them in."

Brock couldn't take his eyes off the

woman. "I knew you looked familiar," he said. "You're Nurse Joy!"

"Joy?" the woman asked.

Brock turned to Ash. "It's Nurse Joy — the one whose poster we saw at the wharf."

"Now that you mention it, they do look alike," Misty said.

The woman was confused. "I don't know what you mean," she said. "I have lived in this castle since my birth."

She turned away. "Please follow me."

Ash and the others followed her down the long dock. New Island was rocky and covered with gray boulders. A tall tower topped by a windmill sat in the middle of the island.

"That must be Pokémon Palace," Ash said.

"Some palace," Misty said. "It looks more like a haunted castle."

Ash thought Misty was right. This place was definitely creepy.

The dock led to a tunnel cut into the rock. The woman's lantern barely lit up the dark passageway. Slimy water dripped from the tunnel walls.

"What are we getting into?" Misty asked in a harsh whisper.

"I don't know," Ash said. "But we'll find out soon enough."

Soon the lantern shone on two large gray doors. Ash jumped back as the doors swung open in front of them.

The doors revealed a large, long hall. A huge banquet table filled the center of the room. A spiral staircase curved up to the top of the tower. Torches on the walls cast a bright glow.

Three Pokémon trainers sat at the table. Ash recognized them from the wharf.

"Now all the trainers worthy of an audience with my master have arrived," the woman said.

"Only three?" Misty asked. "But there were so many at the wharf."

"Only the trainers capable of braving the storm have proven themselves worthy in my master's eyes," the woman said.

Brock looked thoughtful. "Do you mean the storm was a test?"

The woman ignored him. "Let your

Pokémon out of their Poké Balls and have a seat," she said. "You are chosen trainers."

"Chosen for what?" Ash asked, but the woman walked out of the room.

Ash shrugged. "I guess we'll know soon." He took a Poké Ball from his belt and released his Bulbasaur. Brock released his Vulpix, a reddish-brown Fire Pokémon that looked like a fox.

Misty released her Psyduck, a yellow Water Pokémon that waddled like a duck.

They stepped into the hall.

"So you made it, too," said one of the trainers.

Ash recognized him as Fergus, the trainer who had argued with the wharfmaster.

The other trainer spoke up, the skinny one with the messy hair.

"I'm Corey. I made it, too," he said. "A hurricane is a breeze for my Pidgeotto."

Corey pointed to Pidgeotto, who flew over to a group of Pokémon. Corey also had a Venusaur, the most evolved form of Bulbasaur. There was Hitmonlee, a Fighting

Pokémon with a powerful kick. He also had a Sandslash, a Ground Pokémon; a Rhyhorn, which looked like a rhinoceros; and a Scyther, a Flying Bug Pokémon with sharp, curved claws.

"Wow," Ash said. "That's a nice Pokémon collection."

Fergus interrupted. "Well, *I* rode over on my Gyarados. My Pokémon can't be beat."

Ash looked over Fergus's Pokémon. The giant Gyarados floated in a pool with other Water Pokémon: Golduck, the evolved form of Psyduck; Tentacool, a Poison Water Pokémon; Vaporeon, the evolved Water form of a Pokémon called Evee; and Seadra, a Pokémon that looked like a powerful sea horse. Rounding out the group of Water Pokémon was a Nidoqueen, a Ground Pokémon with a mean, poisonous sting.

The third trainer walked up and shook Ash's hand. She was the brown-haired girl from the wharf. "I'm Neesha," she said. "I crossed the storm on my Dewgong. These are my Pokémon."

Neesha had a puffy pink Wigglytuff, which could sing a mysterious song; a Blastoise, the evolved form of Squirtle; and a Vileplume, a Poison Grass Pokémon that looked like a mushroom or a flower. She also had some of the world's most beautiful Pokémon: a furry white Ninetales with nine bushy, flowing tails; and a Rapidash, a white horselike Pokémon with a flaming mane and tail.

"That's a great collection, too." Ash was impressed. Inside, he was also a little nervous. Was he going to have to battle all these trainers? He knew they would be tough to beat. And what about this world's greatest Pokémon trainer? Could Ash beat him, too? He wasn't so sure.

The woman from the hologram stepped back into the room.

"Sorry to have kept you waiting," she said. "The world's greatest Pokémon trainer will now make himself known."

Suddenly, a bright light illuminated a large tube at the end of the room. Blue fluid filled the tube.

The Pokémon in the room tensed for battle. Pikachu and Togepi hid behind Ash's legs.

Ash watched in amazement as a figure floated down the tube. The figure didn't look human at all.

It looked like a Pokémon.

The Pokémon floated out of the bottom of the tube and landed gently on the ground. It was a tall, catlike Pokémon with powerful muscles in its arms and legs and a long, curved tail.

"A Pokémon? It can't be," the trainers muttered.

"Meet the world's strongest Pokémon trainer — *and* the world's most powerful Pokémon," the woman announced. "This is Mewtwo."

Chapter Seven

Mewtwo's Psychic Power

"Mewtwo," Ash repeated. He stared in awe at the powerful Pokémon.

Fergus rose from his chair. "A Pokémon can't be a Pokémon trainer! This is ridiculous!"

"Is that so wrong?" Mewtwo said calmly. As Mewtwo spoke, the woman spoke the same words at the same time.

It's like she's under Mewtwo's control, Ash thought, amazed. *She's like a puppet.*

Mewtwo glared at Fergus. The Pokémon's eyes glowed with a bright blue light. Mewtwo aimed the light at Fergus.

The blue light surrounded Fergus, then lifted the trainer high into the air.

The other Pokémon trainers gasped in amazement.

Carried by the blue light, Fergus floated higher and higher to the ceiling.

"Let him down!" Ash demanded.

Mewtwo whirled his head around. In a flash, the blue light sent Fergus spinning across the room. With a splash, he landed in a pool with his Water Pokémon.

Fergus stood up.

"So you're using psychic power, are you?" Fergus said. "No problem. Gyarados, attack!"

The gigantic Pokémon lifted its long neck from the pool and faced Mewtwo.

"Gyarados, Hyper Beam!" Fergus commanded.

Gyarados opened its large mouth. A powerful beam of golden yellow light shot out. The Pokémon aimed the full force of the beam at Mewtwo.

Mewtwo calmly held out one hand. It

Mewtwo, the most powerful
Pokémon ever created!

A clone of the legendary Pokémon Mew, Mewtwo was created by scientists in a lab. But it's not planning on *staying* a test subject!

An ancient stone carving of Mew.

Mewtwo escapes the lab — by setting it on fire!

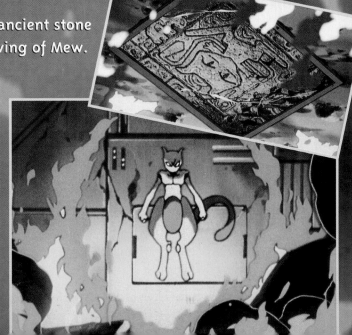

Impressed by Ash's skills in Pokémon battle, Mewtwo sends Dragonite to invite Ash, Misty, and Brock to a "party" for promising trainers on New Island.

Bulbasaur shows its strength in a Pokémon match.

Gyarados crosses the stormy sea.

Team Rocket decides to crash Mewtwo's party — despite the bad weather!

Meanwhile, Mew — the legendary Pokémon — appears far beneath the sea . . .

. . . then decides to join Team Rocket as they explore New Island.

Brock, Ash, Pikachu, Misty, and Togepi are led onto
the island by a woman who looks a lot like Nurse Joy.

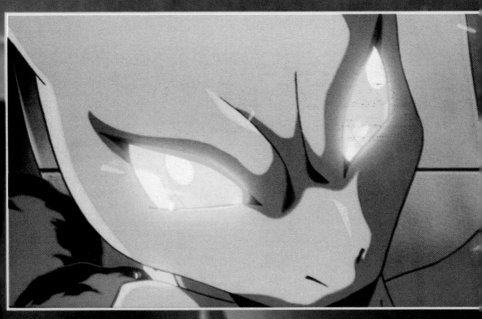

Mewtwo shows off its psychic powers to the Pokémon trainers: "Meet the world's strongest Pokémon trainer — *and* the world's most powerful Pokémon!"

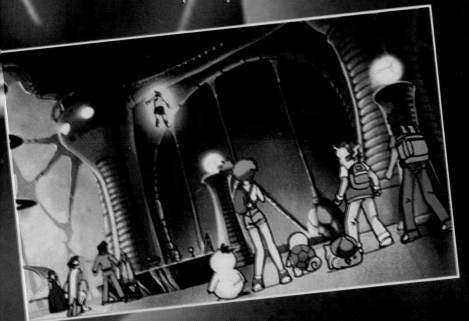

Mewtwo uses special black-and-silver Poké Balls to
capture the trainers' Pokémon — and clone them!

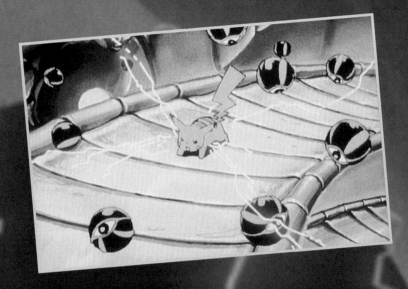

Pikachu uses its electric shock powers to keep the Poké Balls away — but it can't hold them off forever!

Ash leads the Pokémon originals against
Mewtwo's army of clones.

Meowth vs. Meowth — and Charizard vs. Charizard!
Who will win — the originals or the clones?

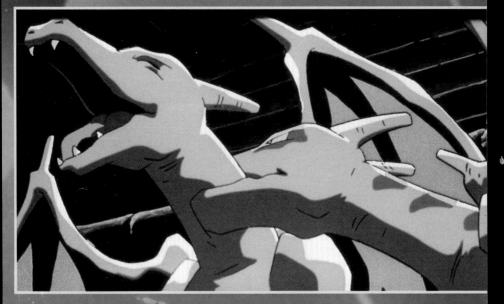

Mew and its clone face off in midair!

Realizing that the Pokémon and their clones are
destroying each other, Ash tries to stop Mewtwo —
but gets caught in the crossfire! Will Ash survive?

Moved by Pikachu's love, all the Pokémon —
originals and clones — cry for Ash. And magically,
their tears revive him!

Together, Ash and Pikachu prove that humans and Pokémon — originals or clones — can live in peace and harmony.

caught the beam and reflected it right back at Gyarados.

Slam! The beam collided with the giant sea serpent. Gyarados toppled over, crashing into the pool with a loud splash.

A hush filled the room.

Mewtwo has just defeated one of the most powerful Pokémon in the world, Ash thought. *Gyarados couldn't even fight back.*

Mewtwo looked at the fallen Gyarados with satisfaction. Then it turned and raised a hand behind the woman who had been assisting him.

"I have no further need of you," Mewtwo said coolly.

The woman reeled, then collapsed to the floor in a heap. Brock ran to her side. Her hat slipped to the ground, revealing her full face for the first time.

"Nurse Joy," Brock said. "It *is* you!"

Nurse Joy glanced around the room with a dazed look in her eyes. "Where am I?" she asked. "What am I doing here?"

Mewtwo spoke. "I brought you from the Pokémon Center to help me here. Having someone around who knew Pokémon physiology was very convenient. You have been quite useful. But you don't remember a thing, do you?"

Nurse Joy shook her head.

Brock stood up. He looked angry. "What gave you the right to do this to her?"

Mewtwo shrugged. "I am the most powerful creature in the world. I can manipulate humans as I please."

A chill ran down Ash's spine.

Mewtwo was the most powerful creature he had ever seen.

He wasn't sure what Mewtwo was planning to do.

He wasn't sure if he could stop it, either.

Chapter Eight

Team Rocket's Discovery

While Ash and the others faced Mewtwo in the tower, Mew, the legendary Pokémon from the pink bubble, reached New Island after journeying from its peaceful home. Curious, Mew flew around the tower.

The blades of the windmill moved gently. Mew stared, fascinated. Smiling, Mew hopped on the moving blades.

Mew wasn't the only new visitor to the island. A few minutes earlier, Jessie, James, and Meowth — Team Rocket — had washed up on the shore.

James struggled to his feet. Water dripped from his hair.

"Team Rocket has made it once again!" he said. "Now let's go surprise all of those Pokémon trainers and their wonderful Pokémon."

Jessie and Meowth followed James along the rocky coast to the base of the tower. Two large metal doors marked an entrance.

Jessie pulled at the doors.

"They're locked!" Jessie said. "There's no way in."

"Yes, there is," James said. He pointed to a hole above them in the tower wall. Water trickled from the hole. It looked like some kind of sewer or drainage pipe.

"Count me out!" Meowth said. "I'm no river rat."

"Quit complaining," Jessie scolded.

Team Rocket scaled the tower wall. Flying behind them, Mew watched like a curious kitten.

Mew followed as Jessie, James, and Meowth crawled into the hole. The pipe was wide enough for them to stand up. James took a flashlight from his belt.

He led the way as they walked through the dark pipe. Soon, James's flashlight illuminated a ladder on the wall.

"This looks like a way in," Jessie said. "Let's go!"

Team Rocket climbed up the ladder. A round metal plate covered a hole in the ceiling above them. Jessie pushed the heavy plate aside, and they hoisted themselves up through the hole.

Team Rocket gazed at the dimly lit room. Computers and strange-looking machines lined the walls. But strangest of all was a giant machine in the center of the room. A long conveyor belt led from a hole in the wall into a metal chamber filled with mechanical hands. The metal chamber led into an even bigger chamber that looked like a coiled snail shell. Several tubes filled with blue-green fluid snaked out of the machine like glass tendrils.

"What is this place?" Meowth asked.

Jessie and James were too stunned to

answer. They got closer to the tubes. Inside three of the tubes were Pokémon — sleeping Pokémon.

"This one's a Venusaur," Meowth said.

"Here's a Blastoise," said Jessie.

James stood in front of one tube. It held a Flying Pokémon that looked like a large lizard. "This one looks like a Charizard," James said. "At least, I think so. I've never seen Pokémon in this condition before."

Jessie backed away from the tubes. "Maybe we should try to find — whoa!"

Jessie stumbled backward onto a computer keyboard. A large computer screen flashed on behind her. James and Meowth gathered around the screen. Mew flew behind them, unseen.

A strange-looking machine appeared on the screen. It looked like the machine in the room.

"I am recording this message from the Pokémon cloning laboratory on New Island," said a voice from the computer. "This machine you see was created to make copies of Pokémon — clones."

The picture of the machine faded from

the screen. A photo took its place. It looked like an ancient cave drawing. It was a small, catlike Pokémon. Team Rocket had never seen it before.

The computer voice continued. "For our first copy, we used a fossilized eyebrow from the legendary Pokémon, Mew. The eyebrow was discovered deep in the jungles of the Amazon."

"What's a Mew?" Meowth wondered.

"We used Mew's DNA to create a new Pokémon, Mewtwo. But the copy we produced was far from normal. Mewtwo was too powerful . . . and incredibly violent. No one can stop it! We must leave the castle immediately."

Static clouded the picture on the screen. Then the screen faded to black.

"So this is the laboratory that was destroyed?" Jessie asked.

"If it is, then who fixed it?" asked James.

Meowth kicked the computer. "This piece of junk isn't good for — hey, wait!"

The computer screen flashed back on. A whirring sound filled the room as the machine came to life. Two mechanical hands reached out and grabbed Meowth. They dropped the Pokémon onto the conveyor belt.

"Oh, no!" James cried. He leaped onto the conveyor belt and grabbed Meowth. Jessie grabbed onto James. Together they pulled Meowth out of the clutches of the mechanical hands.

"Ouch!" Meowth cried. The hands pulled three hairs from Meowth's tail. "My hair! Give it back!"

Team Rocket whirled around as the voice on the computer continued.

"Only a small amount of Pokémon DNA is needed to make a copy," said the voice.

Three hairs appeared on the computer screen.

"Those hairs," Jessie said, "I think they're Meowth's!"

The image of the hairs faded. Now a picture of a Pokémon appeared.

A Meowth.

"I don't like this one bit," Meowth grumbled.

Another whirring sound filled the room. One of the tubes attached to the machine began to glow brightly. Team Rocket watched as a small Pokémon popped out of the machine and into the tube. The Pokémon floated down the tube and rested at the bottom.

Jessie, James, and Meowth ran to the tank.

A sleeping Meowth floated in the blue-green fluid.

"I'm having double vision!" James cried.

"It's a copy of Meowth!" Jessie exclaimed.

Meowth covered its eyes. "It can't be!" Meowth moaned. "I've been cloned!"

The Three Clones

In the room above the lab, Mewtwo faced the trainers and their Pokémon.

Corey stepped up to Mewtwo.

"You are a Pokémon," he said. "You must respect humans."

Mewtwo looked at Corey scornfully. "Humans created me. Some wanted to test me. Another wanted me to serve him. But I will serve no human. I am more powerful than any of you."

"So you think Pokémon are better than humans?" Brock asked.

Mewtwo shook its head. "Pokémon are no good, either. They have allowed humans to rule this world. They have allowed themselves to become servants."

Pikachu ran out from behind Ash. *"Pika! Pika! Pika!"* Pikachu said excitedly.

Mewtwo translated Pikachu's words. "You say you're not a servant. You're with your trainer because you want to be?"

"Pika pi!" Pikachu replied.

Mewtwo looked thoughtful for a moment. Then its face clouded. It glared at Pikachu. "No. You're wrong. You're weak if you need to be with humans."

Mewtwo's eyes glowed with blue light. It aimed a psychic blast at Pikachu. The blast sent Pikachu flying backward. Ash jumped behind Pikachu, stopping its flight. They crashed to the floor.

Misty, Squirtle, and Bulbasaur ran to Ash and Pikachu. Ash slowly sat up. He was stunned but okay. Pikachu was fine, too.

Ash staggered to his feet and faced Mewtwo. "You can't do that to my Pikachu!" he cried.

Corey was angry, too. "If you're a Pokémon, then I can capture you with a Poké-mon!" he yelled. "Go, Rhyhorn!"

The powerful Rhyhorn charged at Mewtwo. Ash had seen this strong creature do incredible damage with its massive limbs and its long, sharp horn.

Mewtwo stood calmly and faced the charge. It grabbed Rhyhorn's horn in one hand. Then it hurled Rhyhorn backward. The beast crashed into the banquet table and thudded to the floor.

"Rhyhorn!" Corey cried. He ran to his Pokémon's side.

"It's no use," Mewtwo said. "I was born stronger than any Pokémon on this planet."

"There's only one way to find out if that's true," Ash said.

"Are you sure you *want* to find out?" countered Mewtwo.

Ash stood firm. "You bet I do!"

"Fine," Mewtwo said. A blue glow sur-rounded its head.

In the laboratory below, Team Rocket watched as the tubes began to glow with blue light. Behind them, Mew watched, too.

All at once, the sleeping Pokémon clones began to stir.

Blastoise was the first to open its eyes. The bottom of the tube opened up and deposited Blastoise onto the floor.

Blastoise stood tall. Two water guns popped out from under its shell.

"Blastoise!" it said in a deep voice.

Next, a Charizard popped out of the tube. This Pokémon looked like an ordinary Charizard, with its wings and long, flaming tail. But its leathery skin was covered with brown zigzags.

The cloned Charizard flapped its wings and shot a blast of fire from its mouth.

Finally, the tube ejected a Venusaur. The huge blue-green beast opened its mouth and let out a mighty roar.

Suddenly, the cloned Pokémon stopped. They turned their heads, as if hearing some unseen voice. Then, one by one, they stomped through the doors of the lab.

Mew watched with interest.

"*Mew!*" it said. The pink Pokémon flew after them — and right past Team Rocket.

Team Rocket watched the lab doors close.

"What just happened here?" asked Meowth.

"I think those were copies of Pokémon made in the lab," Jessie said.

"And that was a Mew — the legendary Pokémon we saw on the computer screen," James added.

"Should we go after them?" Jessie asked.

Meowth answered her. "I think Team Rocket is nice and safe right here!"

Upstairs in the main hall, Ash and the trainers watched in amazement as three large holes in the floor opened up. One by one, the three cloned Pokémon rose to the floor on platforms.

The trainers' Pokémon looked at the copies and shrunk back in fear.

"I have created the evolved forms of the Pokémon that are sought by any would-be Pokémon trainer," Mewtwo explained. "Blastoise is the evolved form of Squirtle.

Venusaur is the evolved form of Bulbasaur. And Charizard is the evolved form of Charmander."

"I've got a Venusaur, too," Corey said. "Its name is Bruteroot."

With a grunt, Bruteroot stepped up to Corey's side.

"And don't forget my Blastoise, Shellshocker," Neesha said.

Shellshocker stepped up next to Neesha, its water guns ready to go.

Ash threw a Poké Ball. "And it may not have a nickname, but I've got a Charizard."

Ash's Charizard appeared in a blaze of light.

Charizard took one look at Mewtwo and shot a powerful blast of fire from its mouth right at the Pokémon.

Mewtwo didn't move. The flames surrounded Mewtwo, then instantly turned to ice. The icicles clattered harmlessly to the floor.

"Char!" said Charizard with frustration.

"Charizard, I didn't give you any battle commands yet!" Ash said. No matter how hard he tried, Ash couldn't control this

Pokémon. Sometimes Charizard obeyed him, but most of the time it didn't.

Mewtwo waved its hand. The wall behind dissolved to reveal a huge Pokémon gym outside the hall. The gym filled a huge open courtyard in the center of Pokémon Palace. Electric lights illuminated the battle lines on the gym floor.

"Enough games," Mewtwo said with a snarl. "Let's see what your Pokémon can do."

Chapter Ten

The First Battle

Mewtwo and the cloned Pokémon Blastoise, Venusaur, and Charizard lined up at one end of the gym.

At the other end, Corey stood next to Bruteroot, his Venusaur. Neesha stood next to Shellshocker, her Blastoise. And Ash stood next to his Charizard. Misty, Brock, and the others watched from the sidelines.

"So who will be my first opponent?" Mewtwo asked.

Corey stepped forward.

"I was overconfident before," Corey admitted, "but this time I'm ready. Bruteroot, go!"

Bruteroot stomped to the center of the gym. Mewtwo's cloned Venusaur stomped out and faced it.

"Bruteroot, Razor Leaf!" Umio commanded.

The giant green leaves attached to Bruteroot's back spun off and whipped around in the air. They flew at the cloned Venusaur with tremendous force.

"Venusaur, Vine Whip!" Mewtwo ordered.

Two thick green vines shot out from the plant bulb on top of the cloned Venusaur's back. The vines pushed the attacking leaves out of the way. Then they reached out and surrounded Corey's Bruteroot.

Bruteroot struggled to break the grip of the vines. They were too strong. Mewtwo's Venusaur used the vines to throw Bruteroot across the gym. It hit the wall with a sickening thud.

"There is no way you can win," Mewtwo bragged. "I have engineered these Pokémon so that their special attacks are more powerful than those of ordinary Pokémon."

Neesha stepped into the battle area.

"We'll see about that," she said. "Go, Blastoise!"

Mewtwo pointed to its cloned Blastoise.

The creatures thumped out into the center of the gym and faced each other.

"Shellshocker, Hydro Pump!" Sweet ordered.

Forceful blasts of water shot from the water cannons on Neesha's Blastoise. Before the blast could do any damage, Mewtwo called out, "Skull Bash!"

Mewtwo's Blastoise began to spin around like a giant wheel. The cloned Blastoise spun faster and faster. It tore through the water blast with ease. Then Mewtwo's Blastoise collided with Shellshocker, sending it sprawling to the ground.

Shellshocker was out of the battle.

"Two down," Ash said, more determined than ever. "And one to go! Charizard, go!" Ash called out.

"Be careful, Ash," Misty warned. "Mewtwo's Pokémon attacks are powerful."

"Power won't get you anywhere without speed," Ash said. "Charizard, use your speed attacks!"

Ash felt hopeful as his Charizard obeyed him for once and flew into the air. Mewtwo's Charizard followed.

Ash's Charizard aimed a Fire Blast from its mouth. Mewtwo's Charizard quickly dodged the blast.

"Char!" With a roar, Ash's Charizard aimed another blast. Mewtwo's Charizard dodged it once again.

The two Charizard seemed to dance in the air. As soon as one would attack, the other would evade it. Higher and higher they flew, until finally they took their battle above the clouds.

Ash peered up at the dark sky. It was impossible to tell who was winning. In fact, neither was.

Weakened, the two Pokémon began to descend. Now they were slamming into each other in midair.

The two Charizard collided forcefully one last time. They spiraled back down to the gym floor. Mewtwo's Charizard landed on top of Ash's Charizard as they slammed into the gym floor.

This impact was too much for Ash's Charizard. It lay on the floor, stunned. Ash ran up to it to make sure it was all right.

Mewtwo's Charizard flapped its wings and roared proudly.

"It looks like your speed isn't good enough, either," Mewtwo crowed. "As the winner, I now claim my prize . . . your Pokémon!

"Hey, wait! You can't do that!" Ash shouted.

Mewtwo ignored him and raised its arms. Three Poké Balls appeared in the air. They didn't look like any Poké Balls Ash had ever seen before. They were black and silver.

At Mewtwo's silent command, the Poké Balls flew across the gym.

The first Poké Ball hovered over Corey's fallen Venusaur. In an instant, Bruteroot was captured by a beam of red light.

The second Poké Ball flew to Neesha's

Blastoise. In an instant, Shellshocker was gone.

"No!" Ash cried. He frantically reached for the third Poké Ball.

He was too late. A beam of red light shot out and captured his Charizard.

The three Poké Balls swiftly flew out of the gym.

Mewtwo raised its arms again. Instantly, the gym was filled with silver-and-black Poké Balls.

Misty held Togepi tightly. "You're going to steal our Pokémon!" she cried.

"Steal?" Mewtwo snickered. "No, I'm just going to use them to make stronger copies. Copies that are worthy of me."

"But that's against the rules!" Ash protested.

"This is my world now. I make my own rules," Mewtwo said firmly.

A blast of blue light shot from Mewtwo's eyes. The blast sent Ash flying through the gym. He thudded to the floor.

There was no stopping Mewtwo.

With a wave of Mewtwo's arms, the Poké Balls flew through the air.

At first the Pokémon tried to fight them.

Fergus's Gyarados snapped at the Poké Balls with its sharp teeth.

Zap! Gyarados was captured.

Corey's Pidgeotto flew right at the balls, poised to attack.

Zap! Pidgeotto was captured.

Neesha's Dewgong tried to head-butt the Poké Balls as they flew at it.

Zap! Dewgong was captured.

One by one, the Pokémon in the room were captured by Mewtwo's Poké Balls.

Weakened by Mewtwo's attack, Ash slowly stood up. He frantically searched the gym for his Pokémon.

In one corner he spotted Squirtle and Bulbasaur putting up a brave fight. Squirtle was repelling the Poké Balls with sharp blasts of water squirted from its mouth. Bulbasaur was hitting the Poké Balls with vines that lashed from the plant bulb on its back.

Suddenly, Ash had an idea.

"I've got it!" He took two Poké Balls from his belt. "Squirtle! Bulbasaur! Everyone, get back in your Poké Balls!"

Red light shot from Ash's Poké Balls and safely captured Squirtle and Bulbasaur.

Mewtwo sneered. "It's no use," he said.

Two silver-and-black Poké Balls flew next to Ash.

Zap! They captured the Poké Balls that held Squirtle and Bulbasaur!

Brock ran up to Ash. He carried his Vulpix in his arms.

"It's not going to work, Ash," Brock said. "We've got to run for it!"

Ash nodded.

Brock and Vulpix took off after Misty, who held Togepi tightly in her arms. Psyduck waddled after them.

Together they ran to the entrance doors of the tower. But they just weren't fast enough.

Zap!

"Vulpix!" Brock cried.

Zap!

"Oh, no! My Psyduck!" Misty yelled.

Ash watched helplessly as his friends' Pokémon were captured. Then he whirled around in a panic.

Where was Pikachu?

"Pika!"

Pikachu was running swiftly across the gym. A swarm of Mewtwo's Poké Balls followed it.

"Pikachu! I'm coming!" Ash ran after his Pokémon.

Pikachu ran through the gym and back into the main hall. It charged up the spiral staircase that rose to the highest point in the tower.

Pikachu ran up the staircase. The silver-and-black Poké Balls gained on it. Soon they would be close enough to capture it.

"Pikachu!" Pikachu shot a blast of electricity at the Poké Balls as it ran.

The blast worked — for a second. In an instant, the Poké Balls were back in pursuit.

"Pikachu!" Pikachu shot off another blast.

The blast repelled the Poké Balls — but soon they were right back on Pikachu's trail.

Ash was gaining on Pikachu.

"Hang on, Pikachu! I'm almost there!"

Suddenly, Ash lost his balance. His feet slipped out from under him.

Ash flew off the staircase. Frantic, he grabbed its railing. He dangled hundreds of feet from the floor.

Ash looked up. Mewtwo's Poké Balls crowded around Pikachu.

Ash knew there was nothing he could do.

Pikachu was going to be captured!

Chapter Eleven

The Clones Are
Created

Pikachu ran higher and higher up the staircase, dodging Mewtwo's Poké Balls at the same time.

Pikachu dodged to the left. To the right. Then, suddenly, it lost its balance.

Pikachu plummeted to the floor!

"No!" Ash cried.

Pikachu whizzed by him. Ash let go of the railing.

Ash reached out and tried to grab Pikachu as he fell. He had to save Pikachu somehow.

Mewtwo's Poké Balls dove after Pikachu.

Zap! A silver-and-black Poké Ball captured Pikachu in midair.

Ash grabbed the Poké Ball in one hand. A split second later, he landed in the pool below.

Ash swam to the water's surface. He clutched the ball that held Pikachu.

"I've got you!" he cried triumphantly.

But the ball jerked out of Ash's hands and flew away.

"Not again!" Ash cried.

He charged after the ball, which flew into a hole in the floor of the hall.

Ash dove through the hole into pitch-blackness. He landed with a thud on a conveyor belt that ran through a dark tunnel.

Ash crawled along the conveyor belt. The ball that held Pikachu was just ahead. He had to reach that Poké Ball.

The tunnel opened up into a large laboratory of some kind. Up ahead, the conveyor belt led to a large machine. A machine that looked like a giant snail shell.

The conveyor belt took Pikachu's Poké Ball into a metal chamber.

Ash scrambled into the chamber. Metal hands were clutching the ball. Ash tried to pry the hands away from the ball. More metal hands pulled at his hair and his clothes. They wouldn't let go of the Poké Ball.

"I won't let you down, Pikachu!" Ash cried.

With all his might, Ash pulled at the Poké Ball. He flew backward as the mechanical hands released the ball.

Ash crashed to the floor. The Poké Ball clattered next to him and opened. There was a blaze of light. Then Pikachu was standing in front of him.

"Pika!"

"Pikachu! You're all right!" Ash hugged the Pokémon.

"Ash and Pikachu?"

Ash looked up. Team Rocket was staring at them. They looked a little dazed.

Ash rose to his feet. He looked around the lab.

"What's going on here?" he asked Team Rocket.

Jessie pointed to the computer screen.

"Just look!" she said.

An image of Pikachu flashed on the computer screen. Then a copy of the Pokémon appeared in one of the tubes and floated down into the blue-green fluid.

"So this is how Mewtwo is making his copies!" Ash said.

"It's happening to all of the Poké Balls," James said.

Silver-and-black Poké Balls lined the conveyor belt. As each Poké Ball entered the metal chamber, an image of a Pokémon flashed on the computer screen. Then a copy of the Pokémon appeared in one of the tubes.

Ash looked in terror at the tubes. They were filled with sleeping copies of Pokémon. A Gyarados. A Dewgong. A Pidgeotto.

Even a Pikachu.

Suddenly, the conveyor belt stopped. The machine spit the silver-and-black Poké Balls out onto the floor of the lab.

The Pokémon in the tubes opened their eyes.

"The copies are awake!" Ash cried.

The bottoms of the tubes opened up, depositing the cloned Pokémon onto the floor of the lab.

The creatures looked like they were under a spell. Slowly they turned and walked, stomped, slid, and flew out of the lab.

"Mewtwo has done it," Ash said. "He's copied all of our Pokémon!"

Ash Takes a Stand

As the cloned Pokémon thumped out of the lab, the vibrations sent the pile of silver-and-black Poké Balls crashing to the ground. The Poké Balls opened, releasing the original Pokémon.

"Squirtle!" Squirtle appeared and hugged Ash.

"Bulbasaur!" Bulbasaur stomped over to Ash and frowned.

"It's all right, Bulbasaur," Ash said. "You're okay now."

"Okay?" James whined. "There's nothing okay about all of those copies running around."

The Pokémon gathered around Ash. He stood tall.

"We won't let Mewtwo and the clones take over the world," Ash said firmly. "No matter what it takes."

Ash led the Pokémon out of the lab.

"Fine, then," Jessie said.

"Good luck, Ash," James said. "We'll just wait here."

In the gym above them, Mewtwo and his Venusaur, Blastoise, and Charizard faced Misty, Brock, Nurse Joy, and the other trainers.

Mewtwo waved its arms. Two doors opened on either side of the gym. Outside, the storm still raged.

"Humans," Mewtwo said, "I will spare your lives. Return now, if you can brave the storm."

"We're not going anywhere!" Misty said. "Why are you doing this? Why do you want to make copies of all our Pokémon?"

"Ordinary Pokémon are too weak," Mewtwo explained. "They live to serve humans. I must create cloned Pokémon like myself. Superior Pokémon that don't depend on humans. Together we will eliminate humans and Pokémon and inherit the world."

Brock glared angrily at Mewtwo. "We won't let you get away with this!"

"As you wish," Mewtwo said. "Let's see if you can stop me and my powerful Pokémon copies."

Behind Mewtwo, the stone floor exploded in a shower of dust and smoke. Through the smoke came the cloned Pokémon.

The trainers gasped in horror. These Pokémon were identical to their own Pokémon. But there was something about them. Something stronger. Something meaner.

The Pokémon gathered behind Mewtwo. Mewtwo looked like a general commanding an army.

"We are ready now," Mewtwo said. "Ready to take control of the planet!"

"Not so fast, Mewtwo!"

Ash stepped out of the dust and smoke.

Pikachu, Squirtle, and Bulbasaur walked at his side. Behind them were all of the original Pokémon.

"Ash!" Misty and Brock cried together.

Ash faced Mewtwo.

"I won't let you do this," he said defiantly.

"So you let them out," Mewtwo said. "A minor inconvenience."

Ash ran straight at Mewtwo. "I'll battle you myself!" he cried.

Ash aimed a powerful punch at Mewtwo's body. A glowing blue light surrounded Mewtwo. The light protected Mewtwo. The punch never made contact.

"Ash, stop!" Misty called out.

Ash wouldn't listen. He charged at Mewtwo again.

The shield of blue light shone brighter.

Ash hit the shield. The shield threw Ash back and up, up into the air.

Ash hurled backward toward a stone ledge high on the tower wall.

"Pika!" Pikachu covered its eyes.

Ash braced for the impact.

Instead of hard stone, he hit something soft.

"Huh?" Ash looked down. He had been saved. Saved by a giant pink bubble.

A small, catlike Pokémon floated in the air in front of him.

The Pokémon smiled.

"Mew!" it said.

Chapter Thirteen

Mew

Mew giggled and popped the bubble supporting Ash. Ash fell safely onto the stone ledge.

Down below, Mewtwo glared up at them.

"*It's you,*" Mewtwo growled.

"*Mew,*" the smaller Pokémon replied.

"What is it?" Ash called down.

"It is Mew, the legendary Pokémon," Mewtwo said. "Supposedly the only one of its kind on Earth. And the most powerful Pokémon alive."

Mew gently floated in the air. "*Mew.*

Mew," it said. Ash knew it was talking to Mewtwo.

Mewtwo listened, then grew angry. "But *I'm* the most powerful Pokémon!" Mewtwo protested. "I may have been made from your DNA, but I am the stronger one."

"*Mew.*"

"Mew . . . and Mewtwo," Ash said. "I get it! Mewtwo is a clone of Mew."

Mewtwo's eyes flashed angrily. "We will soon find out who is stronger," Mewtwo said. "I will battle you!"

Mew giggled. Another large pink bubble appeared in the air. Mew happily bounced on the bubble, ignoring Mewtwo.

Mewtwo grew furious. It raised its hand. A glowing black ball of psychic energy appeared. Silver sparks shot from the energy ball.

Mewtwo hurled the energy ball at Mew, bursting the pink bubble. Mew somersaulted in the air.

But Mew only laughed.

Mewtwo raised its arms again. Another energy ball zapped to life. Mewtwo hurled the ball at Mew. Mew dodged the ball, laughing playfully.

That made Mewtwo even angrier. *Whoosh!* Mewtwo hurled another psychic energy ball. And another. And another.

Mew dodged them all.

Ash watched the battle in amazement.

Mew is so small, Ash thought. *But Mewtwo is powerless against it so far.*

Mewtwo flew into the air and lunged at Mew.

It couldn't catch Mew. The smaller Pokémon refused to fight. It zigged and zagged around Mewtwo, avoiding Mewtwo's attacks.

"Why won't you fight?" Mewtwo asked. "Are you afraid to battle me?"

Mew just laughed.

Raging now, Mewtwo hurled another energy ball at close range.

This one hit its target.

The ball slammed into Mew, sending the Pokémon flying into the clouds.

For a second, the room was quiet.

Mewtwo floated back to the ground. It

stood at the head of the gym with a look of triumph on its face.

Then a sound like a small airplane filled the gym. A flaming ball of fire came hurtling down from the sky. Mew flew behind it.

"Mew reflected the energy ball back at Mewtwo!" Ash exclaimed.

The energy ball shot right at Mewtwo. Quickly, the Pokémon protected itself with a large blue bubble.

Mew floated in the air in front of Mewtwo.

"So you *do* have a little fight in you," Mewtwo said. "Now we'll decide which of us is stronger, my powerful copies or your pitiful Pokémon. The future of the world is at stake. Who will rule — my race of super Pokémon with me as their king, or your spineless Pokémon and their heartless masters?"

"*Mew*," Mew began to talk to Mewtwo. "*Mew, mew.*"

Jessie, James, and Meowth popped out of a hole in the floor. Meowth listened with interest to what Mew was saying.

"What did it say?" James asked.

"Mew says that it's not a fair fight because the copies have stronger special powers than the real Pokémon," Meowth translated. "But Mew says that if the Pokémon fight hand to hand, without using any special attacks, the real ones won't lose to the copies. A real Pokémon's strength comes from the heart."

"But how can Mewtwo and Mew stop the Pokémon from using their special attacks?" Jessie asked.

Meowth listened. "Mew says that it and Mewtwo will use their psychic powers to control the Pokémon during the battle. They will make sure the Pokémon don't use any special attacks."

On the gym floor, Mewtwo stood tall. "You think you are better than us because you came first," it told Mew. "But we are better because we are stronger. We can defeat you even without using special attacks."

Mewtwo opened its arms wide. The cloned Pokémon lined up behind it, ready to battle.

"We'll see which of us is better," Mewtwo said. "Let the battle begin!"

Chapter Fourteen

Fight to the Finish

A terrible cry filled the air as the two Pokémon teams rushed at each other in the center of the gym.

Ash watched the battle from his perch high on the stone ledge.

The two Blastoise faced off, matching each other punch for punch. They fought so intensely that they backed into a corner.

The two Charizard went head to head, each trying to make the other back off first.

The two Bulbasaur roared and fiercely butted heads.

The two Nidoqueen stabbed at each other with their sharp nose horns.

The two Hitmonlee aimed kicks at each other with their powerful legs.

With its fangs bared, Mewtwo's Gyarados bit at the long neck of Fergus's Gyarados.

Ash looked for his Pokémon. "Squirtle! Bulbasaur! Be careful!" he called out.

Down below, Ash's Squirtle wrestled with the cloned Squirtle on the gym floor. The two Bulbasaur fiercely slammed into each other.

Two Scythers dueled with their sharp, curved claws.

Even Misty's Psyduck entered the battle. It and Mewtwo's Psyduck exchanged slaps.

Mew floated above the fray, protected by its pink bubble. Mewtwo held out its arms, and its shimmering blue bubble surrounded it.

The bubbles flew high into the sky. Sparks of psychic energy crackled in the air.

The bubbles charged at each other with

full force. They slammed together in the air, then flew apart, ready for the next attack.

Ash looked down on the scene, a sick feeling in his stomach.

Where's Pikachu in all this? Ash wondered. *I hope it's okay.*

Down below, Pikachu was running toward the ledge.

"*Pikachu!*" the Pokémon called out to Ash.

Ash spotted it. "Hang on, Pikachu!" he called out.

Suddenly, Pikachu stopped in its tracks. Something was blocking its path.

It was the cloned Pikachu.

The cloned Pikachu glared angrily at Ash's Pikachu. Electric sparks flew from its face.

"*Pikachu!*" Mewtwo's Pikachu said angrily. It wanted to fight.

Ash's Pikachu shook its head. "*Pika, pika.*"

Ash watched his Pikachu from high on the ledge. He understood what Pikachu meant. Pikachu didn't want to fight its clone.

Ash began to panic. *I have to help Pikachu. If it won't fight, its clone will destroy it.*

He looked for a way to get down. The wall of the tower was dotted with other stone ledges. If he could climb from one to another, he might be able to make it down. But the stone between the ledges was smooth — there was almost nothing to grab on to.

"Pika!" A cry of pain floated up to the ledge. Ash looked down. The cloned Pikachu delivered a powerful punch to Ash's Pikachu.

"I'm coming, Pikachu!" Ash cried. He took a deep breath and began to back down the ledge. He searched for a foothold in the smooth wall. A small piece of rock jutted out. Ash stepped gingerly on the rock.

Crack! His weight was too much for the foothold. Ash slid down the tower wall and tumbled onto a small ledge below. His head hit the rock with a thud.

Down below, the battling Pokémon exchanged blow after blow.

The two Pidgeotto pecked at each other with their beaks.

The two Ninetales pawed at each other's faces.

All of the battling Pokémon looked exhausted.

From the sidelines, Nurse Joy looked on the creatures with pity. "What's the point of this battle?" she said. "It doesn't matter which Pokémon are better or stronger. They're all alive!"

Brock nodded. "They're too evenly matched — they'll never be able to beat each other."

Misty looked at the battle sadly. Togepi peeked out from its safe place in Misty's backpack.

"This is terrible," Misty said. "There won't be any winners in this battle. Only losers. All this proves is that fighting is wrong."

On the other side of the gym, Team Rocket watched the fight.

"I was prepared for trouble . . . but not for this," James said.

"Make that double . . . for me. It's so awful," Jessie said.

"They're all hurting each other," James said.

The cloned Meowth walked up to Team Rocket and faced Meowth.

"It's you," Meowth said. "What do you want?"

The cloned Meowth raised its paws. Its sharp claws popped out.

Meowth bared its claws, too. Then it stopped.

"I can't fight you," Meowth said. "It would be like fighting myself."

The cloned Meowth frowned. *"Meowth,"* it said. *"Meowth, meowth."*

"You say you don't want to fight, either?" Meowth said.

The cloned Meowth nodded. It sighed, then gazed up at the sky.

A full moon shone down on the gym.

"Meowth, meowth," said the cloned Meowth.

Meowth smiled. "You say the full moon is beautiful tonight? I think so, too." Meowth put a paw around its clone. "We have a lot in common. You've got great taste."

The brief moment of peace didn't last long. In the air above them, the battle between Mew and Mewtwo was heating up.

Ash groaned and opened his eyes. The air sparkled with psychic electricity. Mew in its pink bubble and Mewtwo in its blue bubble were whizzing through the air, colliding again and again. Each time was more forceful than the last.

Ash watched as Mew and Mewtwo took their battle up to the top of the tower and out into the clouds above.

Then he remembered.

"Pikachu!" he cried.

Down below, the cloned Pikachu delivered blow after blow to Pikachu's face.

"*Pika pi!*" the cloned Pokémon said angrily. It wanted Pikachu to fight back.

"*Pika pika,*" Ash's Pikachu answered sadly. It wouldn't fight. No matter how badly it was hurt.

"That's enough!" Ash yelled at the cloned Pikachu. "Stop it! Stop the fight!"

Brock heard Ash's cry. "It's no use," he called up to Ash. "The battle will go on as long as Mew and Mewtwo continue fighting."

"But why?" Misty asked.

Nurse Joy answered her. "It's the nature of all Pokémon," she explained. "They will fight until they beat their opponent. They won't give up."

Ash had to get down. He began to climb back down the wall. This stretch was a little easier. He found a strong foothold and made his way to the next ledge.

Ash looked down. He wasn't far from the gym floor now.

"Pikachu, hang on!"

Ash scrambled to the next ledge. He was about ten feet from the floor now. He looked around.

There were no more footholds. No more ledges. There was only one way down.

"I'm coming!" Ash jumped from the ledge and tumbled to the gym floor. He ran to Pikachu's side.

The cloned Pikachu was exhausted. It took one final swing at Ash's Pikachu, then collapsed. Ash's Pikachu caught the exhausted clone in its arms.

Ash hugged his Pikachu. "Pikachu, I'm so sorry!"

Terrible screams and roars filled the gym. All around them, Pokémon were collapsing. They were tired and beaten. They had barely enough energy to stand, but they wouldn't give up the battle.

"This has got to stop!" Ash cried. "We have to stop this!"

Suddenly, Mew and Mewtwo swooped down from the sky in their bubbles. The bubbles crashed onto the gym floor.

Mew floated on one side of the gym. Instead of a pink bubble, it was surrounded by angry pink flames.

Mewtwo faced Mew. Angry blue flames surrounded Mewtwo.

Mew's pink flames began to glow. A powerful psychic charge of white light burst from its body.

Mewtwo's blue flames began to glow. A powerful psychic charge of white light burst from its body.

Ash couldn't stand it anymore. There had been enough destruction.

The battle had to stop.

"Stop!" Ash cried. "No more!"

Ash ran to the middle of the gym floor.

The white blasts came at him from either side.

The blasts collided, causing a huge explosion of white light.

And Ash was trapped in the middle.

The white light dissolved.

For a split second, Ash hung in midair, his body glowing.

Then he fell.

Ash's body lay motionless on the gym floor.

Chapter Fifteen

Pokémon Tears

"Fool," Mewtwo said. "A human trying to stop our battle."

Pikachu rushed up to Ash.

Ash wasn't moving.

"Pikaaaaaaachu!" Pikachu cried. It *had* to bring him back to life! Electric shocks flew from its body and into Ash's body.

But Ash didn't move.

"What's it doing?" Misty whispered.

"Pikachu's trying to revive Ash with its electric power," Brock explained.

"Pikaaaaaaachu!" Pikachu shocked Ash again.

Nothing happened.

"Pikaaaaaaachu!"

Still nothing.

A hush fell across the room.

"Oh, no," Misty sobbed. "Not Ash."

Pikachu began to cry. Tears flowed down its red cheeks.

And then, the strangest thing happened. Around the room, the other Pokémon, even those who'd been battling, all began to cry for Ash.

Both Squirtle — the clone and the real Squirtle — cried for Ash.

The cloned Bulbasaur and the real Bulbasaur cried for Ash.

Ash's Charizard cried for its fallen master. The cloned Charizard sobbed along with it.

Even the two fierce Gyarados cried for Ash.

The Pokémon's tears shimmered like crystals in the dark gym. The tears floated in the air, illuminating the gym with their twinkling lights.

Squirtle tears joined with Bulbasaur tears. Charizard tears joined with Venusaur tears. Gyarados tears joined with Dewgong tears.

All of the Pokémon cried and cried. Their glimmering tears joined together with Pikachu's tears.

Suddenly, the tears began to form a shimmering spiral. The tornado of tears surrounded Ash. Then they disappeared as if by magic into Ash's body.

Ash's body glowed with soft white light.

In the sky above, the storm clouds cleared. A ray of morning sunshine shone on the gym and lit up Ash's still form.

Pikachu watched Ash hopefully.

Ash blinked.

"Pika?" Pikachu held its breath.

Ash sat up.

He was all right!

"Pikachu!" Ash cried. Pikachu ran into his arms.

The Pokémon smiled and cheered.

"Ash!" Misty cried out. She and Brock ran to their friend.

"It was amazing," Brock said. "The Pokémon tears revived you."

Ash looked around the gym. The Pokémon looked happy now. Cloned Pokémon and real Pokémon smiled at one another.

"Does this mean the battle's over?" Ash asked. He looked at Mewtwo.

A single silver tear fell from the Pokémon's eye.

Mew faced Mewtwo. *"Mew. Mew, mew."*

Mewtwo hung its head. "I understand now. It was the tears of the Pokémon. They showed me that Pokémon can create life and save lives, not just destroy them. I was wrong to create Pokémon just for the purpose of destroying others. I see now that the circumstances of one's birth are irrelevant . . . it is what you do with that life that determines who you are."

"Don't forget Ash," Misty said. "He risked *his* life to save the Pokémon."

Mewtwo nodded. "It's possible for all humans and Pokémon to live together in peace and harmony. I know that now."

Mewtwo faced Ash. "You sacrificed yourself to save the Pokémon. Until I met you, I thought all humans were evil. Thank you for showing me that I was wrong."

"No problem," Ash said.

"Mew!" Mew said happily.

Mew and Mewtwo flew into the air.

A bright white light filled the room.

Slowly, the cloned Pokémon floated up into the air. Psychic energy sparkled around them.

Ash watched the sight in amazement. The giant Gyarados clone floated in the air as though it were as light as a feather. The huge Venusaur clone smiled in wonder as the psychic energy lifted it higher and higher. Ash's Pikachu waved at the Pikachu clone. All of the cloned Pokémon looked happily at Mewtwo.

"Where are they all going?" Ash asked.

"We will find somewhere on this earth where we can live peacefully," Mewtwo said. "Somewhere new."

The bright light in the gym grew even brighter as Mew and Mewtwo flew up through the top of the tower and into the blue sky. The cloned Pokémon rose next.

Mewtwo looked down at the humans and their Pokémon.

I will always remember what happened here, Mewtwo thought, *but it might be better if no one were to know about it. I will use my psychic powers to erase the memory of everyone here. I will return them to the last place they were before they came to the island. They won't remember what happened.*

Suddenly, Ash felt an odd tingling in his body. He felt strangely light.

Ash looked at Pikachu. His Pokémon was floating in the air.

Ash looked down at his own feet. He was floating, too!

Ash was stunned. They were all floating. Misty and Togepi. Brock. Nurse Joy. Corey, Fergus, and Neesha. All of their Pokémon were floating, too.

"What's happening?" Ash shouted.

Ash closed his eyes as the white light grew brighter and brighter.

Then his mind went blank.

Chapter Sixteen

A New Beginning

"Where am I?" Ash asked groggily.

Ash looked around. He was standing in a wharf house with Misty, Brock, Pikachu, and Togepi. The house was filled with Pokémon trainers and their Pokémon. A storm was raging across the ocean outside.

Officer Jenny was addressing the crowd.

"The storm is too bad," she said. "No boats will leave the dock. Please leave the wharf and find safe shelter."

Nurse Joy stepped out of the crowd. "We

can open the Pokémon Center as a shelter," she said.

"Isn't she beautiful?" Brock sighed.

Ash was confused. "I still don't get it. What are we doing here?"

Misty shrugged. "We're here because we're here, I guess." She looked confused, too.

Mewtwo had returned them all to the wharf and erased the memory of everyone there.

The Pokémon trainers and their Pokémon were evacuating the wharf. Ash looked out the window at the raging storm.

Strangely, the dark clouds began to leave the sky. The strong wind died down. The ocean waves were now calm.

A bright sun shone in the blue sky.

And there was something else.

A flash of white.

Ash rushed out of the wharf house.

A Pokémon flew in the sky. A Pokémon with no wings. It looked like a small pink cat. White sparkling light trailed behind it as it flew.

The Pokémon disappeared behind a cloud.

Misty, Brock, and Pikachu ran up to Ash.

"What is it, Ash?" Misty asked.

Ash shook his head. "I'm not sure. I thought I saw something in the sky . . . a legendary Pokémon, I think. There's something kind of familiar about it. But I'm not sure."

"Not many people actually get to see a legendary Pokémon, Ash," Brock said. "If that really was a legendary Pokémon you saw, I bet you'll see it again someday."

"You're right," Ash said. "I won't stop searching until I find that legendary Pokémon and become the greatest Pokémon master in the world. Right, Pikachu?"

"Pika!" Pikachu jumped into Ash's arms.

Miles away, Team Rocket found themselves on an island. An island in the middle of the ocean.

Beautiful flowers covered the ground.

Trees laden with delicious fruit grew all around them.

"How did we get here?" Meowth asked.

"I'm not sure," Jessie said. "But there's something familiar about this place, I think."

"Who cares?" James said. "We're in paradise!"

Meowth grinned. "Does this mean that Team Rocket can take a vacation from catching Pokémon?"

"Are you kidding?" Jessie asked. "This place would be even better if we could find some rare Pokémon to bring back to the Boss."

"Like Pikachu, for instance," James said.

"Pikachu, we're coming after you!" Team Rocket shouted together.

About the Author

Tracey West has been writing books for more than ten years. When she's not playing the blue version of the Pokémon game (she started with a Squirtle), she enjoys reading comic books, watching cartoons, and taking long walks in the woods (looking for wild Pokémon). She lives in a small town in New York with her family and pets.